Milo in a Mess

Written and illustrated by
Emma Damon

A & C Black • London

To David, with Love

First paperback edition 2006
First published 2005 by
A & C Black Publishers Ltd
37 Soho Square, London, W1D 3QZ

www.acblack.com

ISBN 0-7136-7422-9

A CIP catalogue for this book is available from the British Library.

A&C Black uses paper produced with elemental chlorine-free
pulp, harvested from managed sustained forests.

Printed and bound in Singapore by Tien Wah Press (Pte) Ltd

Chapter One

Did you know that all polar bears are left-handed? In the morning, they brush their teeth with their left paws.

And then again at night.

They butter their toast with their left paws, too.

Polar bears even write letters with their left paws, not their right.

Milo lived on Polar Bear Island, which
was covered in snow, and had many hills
and caves.

Milo enjoyed exploring the hills and caves with his friends, Jake and Harry, but he felt different from the other bears, and he didn't know why.

When he kicked a football, it didn't go in a straight line.

When he drew
a picture,
nobody
could tell what
it was, and
sometimes he
dropped his
pencil on the floor.

Every morning, Milo skated to Snowy
Vale School with his friends. And every
morning, he would
get in a mess.

Sometimes his long scarf would get tangled up.

Sometimes his red skates would be on the wrong paws.

One day, at school, the class was told to write a poem. But Milo found it difficult to hold the pencil, and his writing came out all wobbly.

"Milo, how messy you are!" said his teacher, Professor Snowball.

And so he became known as 'Messy Milo'.
His friends didn't know the name made
him feel sad. They thought it was funny.

At home, in his cave, Milo sat with his mum around the fire, eating fish soup. "Don't be sad, Milo," said Mum. "Everyone is good at something. You just have to find out what it is."

Milo shook his head, sadly, and went off to bed.

Chapter Two

The next day, Professor Snowball had some exciting news. "We're holding a competition. Every bear must make an animal out of ice. The winner will receive the Golden Snowflake trophy!"

The bears were very excited as they thought about the different sculptures they could make.

Milo was the most excited bear of all.
Maybe this was the chance for him to
be good at something…

But Bully Bear spoiled his thoughts.

Bully was bigger and stronger than Milo
and his friends. During football practice,
Bully would kick the other players so he
could take the ball.

In class, he would tip over an ink bottle to ruin someone's work.
If he got caught, Bully would blame another bear.

"How will you make a sculpture out of ice, Milo?" said Bully Bear. "It will only be a mess. I wouldn't bother trying."

Milo sighed and felt sad. Maybe Bully was right.

Chapter Three

That evening, after eating his fish soup,
Milo decided to go outside for a walk.
"Wrap up warm," said Mum.
Milo put on his scarf and wellies and
went to his secret den.

The den was an old cave. Pine branches hid its entrance. Inside the cave there was a small fire, a lantern and a wooden chair with a soft, blue cushion to sit on.

Milo liked to go there to think quiet thoughts.

Milo sat down and watched the sun set.
A friendly bird came and hopped around
outside the cave.

It was the most beautiful bird Milo had
ever seen. It had multicoloured feathers
and a bright, yellow beak.
"I wonder if I could make that bird
in ice?" thought Milo.

Milo quickly found a block of ice, then
he pulled it into his den and began
to chip away with a chisel.
First he made
the beak…

…and then a wing.

Milo looked at what he had done and frowned. "It doesn't look anything like that beautiful bird. What am I thinking? I'll always be Messy Milo." He threw his chisel on the floor.

As he bent over to pick it up, he cut his left paw. "Ouch!"

Milo wrapped his paw in a bandage.
He would have to use
his right paw now.

Milo began to chip away again.
Strangely, this time it felt easier. Soon,
he had made a beautiful bird.
Milo smiled. How had he managed that?

Suddenly, a bright lantern shone outside the cave. Milo's mum was looking for him. "Milo, what have you been doing? I thought you'd got lost," she said.

"I've been making something for the school competition," said Milo. He took the lantern and shone it on the ice bird. "It's beautiful," whispered Mum. "I made it with my right paw, not my left," said Milo.

Chapter Four

The next morning, Milo's friends came
to collect him for school. They gasped
when they saw the beautiful ice bird.
"That's amazing!" whispered Jake.
"It's much better than mine," said Harry.

At school, all the bears talked about Milo's ice bird. Bully Bear walked off in a sulk. He was not pleased.

Bully had made a fine sculpture too. He thought he was going to win the trophy. Now it sounded like Milo could beat him!

Bully thought of a plan. That afternoon, he sneaked out of school and climbed the hill to Milo's cave. Bully followed a trail of footprints to Milo's den. He went inside and smashed up Milo's ice bird.

Suddenly, Bully heard a noise outside.
It was Milo's mum. Quickly, he ran back
over the hill.

"Ha ha!" Bully chuckled, thinking about
the mess he had made. "Messy Milo won't
win the Golden Snowflake trophy now."

Chapter Five

After school, Milo rushed home to look at his ice bird. Tomorrow was competition day. He really hoped he would win. But when Milo reached his den, all he found was a pool of water.

Milo looked around the den and saw a shiny object on the floor. It was a hammer with the initials B. B. on it. "Bully Bear!" gasped Milo. "He's ruined my ice bird to stop me from winning!"

Milo was very angry. He shook his fists and growled fiercely. This time, Bully would not spoil things for anyone!

Milo marched outside and pulled another block of ice into his den. It was so big, he could barely get it through the door.

Milo picked up his tool with his right paw, and began chipping away again.

He cut a wing
here…

…a beak
there…

…and two large feet.

Milo stayed up all night. His mum
brought him a plate of fish sandwiches
and a bowl of fish soup.

Milo ate quickly, and
then continued chipping away.
Finally, as the sun rose, Milo stood back
to look at his work.

He had made a beautiful new sculpture.
It was a huge ice
eagle, standing
two metres
tall.

Milo smiled happily,
sat down in his chair
and fell into a
deep sleep.

Chapter Six

Two hours later, Milo woke up with a start. It was competition day and he had overslept! Quickly, he put the ice eagle onto his favourite sledge, and pulled it to the top of Icicle Hill.

From there he could see all the sculptures below. There were ice cats and ice dogs, ice giraffes and ice unicorns. Bully Bear had made a wonderful ice rabbit. It was certain to win.

"If only I can get there in time!"
whispered Milo, as he slid down the hill.

Professor Snowball was standing next to Bully's ice rabbit. "And the winner of the Golden Snowflake trophy is…"

Milo let out a loud cry. "Wait for me!"
"Too late," growled Bully angrily.

But everybody else cheered as Milo's sledge came to a stop. The ice eagle was even better than his ruined ice bird.

"Congratulations, Milo," said Professor Snowball. "It's beautiful!"

Milo smiled. "I made it with my right paw, not my left," he said.

Then Professor Snowball announced,
"And the winner of the Golden
Snowflake trophy is … Milo Bear, who we
really can't call Messy Milo any more."

The ice eagle was put in front of the school for everyone to see. Then Milo and his friends celebrated at a party for the rest of the day.

Even Bully joined in. "If Messy Milo can change," he thought, "so can I. And then maybe they won't call me Bully any more."

He went over to Milo. "Congratulations!" he said. "And I'm sorry."
"Thanks," said Milo. "I couldn't have done it without your help!"

Later, at home, Milo went outside and
looked down into the valley. He wanted to
see his beautiful ice eagle again. And, as
he stood there, he was sure he saw it take
off and fly up, up, into the night sky.